Tales From the Drake House Outhouse

Book One

Praise for Storyshares

"One of the brightest innovators and game-changers in the education industry."
– Forbes

"Your success in applying research-validated practices to promote literacy serves as a valuable model for other organizations seeking to create evidence-based literacy programs."
- Library of Congress

"We need powerful social and educational innovation, and Storyshares is breaking new ground. The organization addresses critical problems facing our students and teachers. I am excited about the strategies it brings to the collective work of making sure every student has an equal chance in life."
– Teach For America

"It's the perfect idea. There's really nothing like this. I mean, wow, this will be a wonderful experience for young people."
- Andrea Davis Pinkney, Executive Director, Scholastic

"Reading for meaning opens opportunities for a lifetime of learning. Providing emerging readers with engaging texts that are designed to offer both challenges and support for each individual will improve their lives for years to come. Storyshares is a wonderful start."
- David Rose, Co-founder of CAST & UDL

Tales From the Drake House Outhouse

Book One

Joe Novara

A Storyshares book

Published by Story Share, Inc.

Storyshares

Story Share, Inc.

24 N. Bryn Mawr Avenue #340

Bryn Mawr, PA 19010-3304

www.storyshares.org

Inspiring reading with a new kind of book.

Interest Level: Middle School

Grade Level Equivalent: 2.4

9798885978224

Book design by Storyshares

Storyshares Presents

Chapter One

RAINDROPS EXPLODED ON THE surface of the pond. Lightning crackled then boomed overhead, jump-starting Maddy into a dead run. She lowered her head against the driving rain and ripped her way through the tangled weeds toward a gap-board barn that sagged into the wind.

Was that a leg sticking out of the ground? Maddy slowed for a moment then ran even faster.

Safe inside, she pulled her dripping brown hair straight back, slick as a helmet, then yanked a rubber band from her clenched teeth to cinch her tiny pony tail. She hiked-up her soccer shorts and hauled the sagging knee socks over her long, skinny legs. A curtain of water poured across the barn door. Did she see what she thought she saw? Through the almost constant thunder she heard a muffled cry.

"Hey! Help! Help me!"

Someone was out there. Maddy took a deep breath, ducked under the waterfall, and plunged back into the downpour.

Near a patch of tall weeds, she heard, "I can't get out! Hey!"

Pushing through the spiky stalks, Maddy saw a sandal and shin shoot out of the ground, then disappear. Squatting at the edge of a square hole she was on eye level with a pudgy boy standing waistdeep in a crater. His face was as red as the saggy mop of hair hanging over his ears.

"I know you from school," Maddy said.

"Can we save the introductions for later," the boy asked, "after you help me out of here?"

Maddy reached out a hand and pulled till the boy hooked a knee onto the lip of the hole. One more tug and he was on his belly – muddy, soaked and breathing hard.

By the time they got to the barn, the boy looked less like a chocolate covered Buddha and more like a pile of wet clothes ready for the wash. He flopped onto a removable van-seat propped against a horse stall and flexed his knee. Blood ran down his shin.

"Omigosh," Maddy cried. "You cut yourself."

The boy bent for a close look. "It's only a scratch."

Maddy grabbed her headband and reached it out the barn door under the stream of water pouring off the roof. She squeezed the head band once. Twice. Then she sat next to the boy and cleaned the cut.

"Aren't you in Miss Patterson's room?" the boy asked.

"That was sixth grade. I have Clark this year. Who do you have?"

"Jensen."

They both stared at the driving rain. Maddy spoke first. "How did you end up in the hole? And what are you doing out here, anyhow?"

The boy blushed. "I didn't see the hole... running from the storm..." Jerking his thumb toward the old farm house up a small hill, he added, "My dad's busy restoring that place every weekend and I have to tag along."

Maddy peeked through a slit in the barn siding and studied the two-story, red brick home. Screens fluttered from a sagging porch like tattered sails on a ghost ship. Black plywood hung over a window – a patch over a pirate's blind eye. "Creepy!"

"The Drake House. That's all my dad talks about. Him and his Civil War reenactor buddies."

"Like North and South, Yankees and Rebels, Civil War?"

"You got it. They want to restore this place because it was built around that time and they can have an office and hold their meetings here."

"You mean they're the guys who put on uniforms and shoot guns and have pretend battles, like Gettysburg? Sweet!"

The boy frowned. "Oh, no. Not another one. You like that stuff too?"

"It's history," Maddy said. "We covered the Civil War last year in that unit on slavery. History is fun."

"Not if you have to spend a weekend in a moldy old tent and eat nasty food just because that's what the soldiers did back then. And they make me wear an itchy wool uniform and bang a drum..."

"That sounds cool."

"Boring, is what it is. Maybe if they played paintball, you know, Pop! Pop! Pop! You could tell who shot who. Now, that might be fun. But these guys shoot blanks at each other and decide ahead of time who's going to die and when. And here's me pounding on a stupid drum, pretending I'm enjoying it."

"Like my mom and dad make me play soccer. I hate it. I agree with Einstein."

The boy looked a question at Maddy.

"Einstein – the genius mathematician?"

"I know who Einstein is. What did he say?"

"'Sports are boring. Someone wins and someone loses.'"

The boy snorted. "Only, I always lose. My mom makes me play violin during the week and my dad makes me play soldier when he gets me on weekends." A cell phone chirped in the boy's pocket. He flipped the phone open, walked a few steps away, nodded, nodded again. Then he said, "Me too," and hung up. "My Mom," he explained. "It's like I'm on a leash – a telephone leash."

"So, what exactly do you do out here?"

The boy shrugged. Water ran off his poodle-curly red hair. "Stuff. Like throwing rocks into the pond back there."

"I can see it from the retirement home," Maddy said, pointing to a five story building two fields over, "where my grampa lives. I've always wondered if there were any fish in here."

"There are."

"You sure can't be planning to catch any if you keep throwing rocks at them."

"Catch them?" The boy smiled dreamily. "I'm not trying to catch them. I'm doing research for a fish disaster movie. Animation. There's all these bluegills whizzing around down there, screaming, 'Mom, Mom the sky is falling! It's raining rocks!'"

Maddy looked away, then cut a glance back at the boy.

"And then... and then..." the boy paused. "When it gets cold and the pond freezes in the winter and ice fishermen come out and punch a hole in the ice, the kids all shout, 'Look, Ma – a skylight.' And the mother says 'Don't go near it. Your dad zoomed up through a hole like that and was never seen again.'"

"You're weird," Maddy said.

The boy smiled to himself. "Someday I'm gonna make movies. Somebody has to."

"You come here every Saturday?" Maddy asked.

"You sure ask a lot of questions. But you don't say anything about yourself."

"Maddy. My name is Maddy. I play soccer every Saturday whether I want to or not. My parents are too busy to watch. Grampa takes me."

"You any good?"

"No. I'm kinda slow."

"Me too," Zach admitted, pointing to his short, stubby legs. "So, what happens after the game?"

"I go back to Grampa's place for the rest of the day and sometimes overnight." Maddy smirked. "It's real exciting in a retirement community."

"I have to go to your soccer complex too. Every Saturday morning. My dad's Civil War group runs the concession stand. I have to help. Maybe I'll see you there."

"Anything else you want to know, detective?"

The boy pretended to flip shut a notebook. "That's all for now, ma'am. If you think of anything else between now and next Saturday, give me a call. My name is Zach."

Chapter Two

THE NEXT SATURDAY AFTERNOON Zach pushed through prickly weeds on his way to the pond. The air felt like a bathroom after a shower. Pausing to wipe the sweat from his brow, he spotted Maddy sitting at the water's edge in her soccer uniform: green-white-green-white. Socks, shorts, jersey, head band.

She jerked on a fishing rod. The bobber scooted sideways. Maddy reeled quickly and soon swung a hand-sized bluegill over the sandy shore. Holding the line with the flopping fish on the end, she slid her free hand over the fish's head and down its back to smooth the prickly fins. Once she had a firm grip, she grasped the hook by the shank and pulled it out of the fish's mouth.

"Nice fish!" Zach called.

Maddy jumped. "You scared me."

"Sorry. How many did you catch?"

"Lots. They're really biting."

"Let's see' em."

Maddy gave a blank stare.

"Where's your stringer? Where are all the fish?"

"I don't keep them. I'd have to kill them and clean them and eat them. Besides, I'm a vegetarian," she said, bending down to the water and sliding the fish under the tranquil surface.

Zach gazed at Maddy, shaking his head. "If fish could make a movie about what it's like to be hooked, they'd put someone like you in a hamburger joint. After a while a burger would dangle in front of you. You take a bite and feel a sharp pain in your mouth. Next thing you know, you're flying out of the building. The pain suddenly stops and here's you falling back into the booth. How would you like that? I mean, what's the point?"

"Maybe people would stop eating so much junk food?"

"This is about fish," Zach reminded her. "Try to see this from their point of view."

"Okay. From their point of view," Maddy said. "Would I rather have a sore mouth but live or have a sore mouth and be eaten?"

"How about neither one?"

"How's your leg?" Maddy asked, changing the subject.

"Fine," Zach replied glancing past his belly to the bandage on his knee. "My mom had a fit when I got home. She wanted to know what cut me. Now I do, too. Want to help me find out?"

"Back at the hole?"

"Uh-huh."

Maddy put her fishing rod on the ground and followed Zach. On his belly, reaching his arms into the hole, Zach grunted. "There's something here. I can feel it." He stood and held out a rusty scrap of flat metal. "It's a knife," he said. "It's what cut my knee."

"Doesn't look like a knife to me. How can you tell?"

"See?" Zach pointed out a stubby piece of metal at the end of the blade. "This is the haft, the part that goes into a wooden handle. And the other end, the tip, is broken off."

Zach turned his find over and over, studied it end for end. "I'm going to keep it in the barn," he said. "Hide it. This could be a real antique."

"They probably used it to kill hogs and cows and sheep," Maddy whined, trailing Zach through the waist-high weeds. "Why do they have to kill animals?"

"It's what you do on a farm – raise food. Cows. Chickens. Pigs."

"Milk and eggs are food too, you know," she called to Zach, who was already disappearing into the barn. "And cows and chickens will keep making milk and eggs if you don't go around killing them. And if that knife is as old as you think it is, you should save it for a museum or something."

"Hey, look at this." Zach pointed to a hand-hewn beam. Someone had carved a heart into the wood: *NH + MD forever.*

"So, some guy liked some girl – who knows when," Maddy said.

"NH," Zach muttered. "I wonder who he was. I bet MD was one of the original Drake girls, maybe Mary or better yet – Mariah. Let's say Mariah Drake."

Zach's phone chirped. "I'm all right. Okay?" he pleaded into the mouth-piece. "See you later. Yeah, yeah. Me too."

He snapped the phone shut, stared into space for a long moment, then spoke. "There's a movie here. I'm sure of it. I just have to figure out how to make it happen."

"You don't know anything about this place," Maddy interrupted. "You can't just make up a movie out of nothing. No facts. Just your imagination."

Zach stared at Maddy. His eyes twinkled. "Facts are okay as long as they don't mess up a good story. Besides, history facts don't tell you what people felt and why they did things. That's the fun part – figuring that out. And this place is full of the kind of clues I could use for my movie."

"Like what?" Maddy asked.

"That heart," Zach said, looking up at the beam, "and the knife. Maybe the NH in the heart used it to kill a bear. Or maybe... "

"You're just like my grampa. You two would really get along making up stories from nothing."

"Nothing? This knife isn't nothing. It was part of this farm. Someone used it every day."

"To peel potatoes."

"No imagination," Zach mumbled to himself. "Look, what if...what if this hole is like a dig. You know, where scientists find an ancient site in a desert or something and they dig down layer by layer finding clues about the people who lived back them. The deeper they go, the older the stuff they find." Zach said.

"Now," he continued, "if this knife was at the top of the hole, maybe there are more 'finds' below it. So then, the deeper I go, the closer I get to the first pioneers who settled here. See?"

"Tell you what," Maddy said. "You find more clues and I'll help you save them like in a glass-top box with labels and stuff. But I don't do stories."

"I can't wait to get back in that hole," Zach said. "I bet there's lots of other finds down there and somehow they're going to make a story."

"Don't count on me to pull you out again."

Chapter Three

MADDY WATCHED ZACH LIE face-down, one arm in the hole. She shook her head and wandered toward the house. The side door was covered with plywood as were all the windows. No trespassing. She could hear the workers, Zach's dad and the other volunteers, pounding and sawing inside.

A set of doors angled from the side of the house down to the ground. *It's a storm cellar,* she thought. *Like Dorothy's house in the Wizard of Oz. Auntie Em dragged her there when they saw the tornado coming. But then Dorothy ran back out to get Toto. That kind of storm cellar went down into the basement. I wonder what's down there. I could just go through the house to get to the basement but I'd have to say hello to the men and I'll only be a minute and besides if I find something special...*

Maddy crouched, grabbed the handle with both hands, and hauled on the top door. The hinges groaned like a haunted house till the door was straight up. Then she jumped back and let it fall the rest of the way. Several steps, black with mold, dust and spider webs, disappeared into the gloom below.

Maddy looked around. She saw no one coming and eased down the stairs as if expecting them to crumble or crack. The dirt floor smelled wet and dusty at the same time – like under her friend Neela's front porch after it rained.

As soon as her eyes adjusted to the darkness, she scanned the room. An old broom stood next to the steps. The walls were made of huge stones carefully fitted together. A set of stairs on the left side went up into the house. A wood crate in the corner might have been used to hold potatoes or turnips. A cigar box sat on a shelf above it. Secrets and treasures. Maddy took two steps toward it when she heard voices outside.

"John must have left it open when he brought the lumber in."

"Yeah. I'll get it."

Maddy froze. Before she could think to say, "Hey, I'm down here," the door slammed shut and left her in total darkness. *All right, before I get scared, I've got to find out what's in that box, she thought. Like a kid playing pin-the-tail-on-the-donkey, Maddy held her hands out and slowly slid her feet to locate the crate.*

BUMP.

"Ouch!" Maddy bent to rub her shin then ran her hands up the wall to the shelf. Her fingers patted along the shelf careful to touch the box without knocking it down. She fought the urge to shiver and pull away when she felt small, pill-shaped lumps under her fingers. She tried not to think of the critters that had made the lumps.

A muffled voice called from upstairs, "I'm gonna close up. You guys ready to go?"

She had to hurry. If she couldn't get out the way she came in, she could get locked in for the night. She found the box. Grabbed it. Heard some things rattling inside.

Maddy turned toward the outside stairs and skated along the gritty floor, hoping to feel the steps before crashing into them. When she nudged the bottom stair, she took one step and then raised a hand overhead to feel for the door. She took another careful step and felt the door. She tried to push, but it wouldn't budge. Needing both hands, she set the box on the steps next to her. Using both hands now, she took a deep breath and pushed. The door moved a crack.

"Darn, not enough," she groaned. "I know!" Stooping to avoid hitting her head on the door, Maddy crouched, climbed up one more step, turned to face the basement, pushed her shoulders against the door, and stood slowly. The door raised six inches before she had to let it slam down again.

I need something to prop it open while I go up one more step. The broom.

Maddy repeated her squat-and-lift and this time she propped the broom on the step and jammed the top of the handle against the door while she backed up one more step. As soon as the door was vertical, she shoved it all the way open. Scampering out, she looked around to see if anyone was watching, then she ducked back in for the box, heaved the door shut and scooted for the barn.

Sitting on the van bench, box on her knees, she carefully brushed the dust from the warped cover. La Serena Cigars. A Spanish lady spinning in a red dress. Maddy smiled. *Cool. I wonder what's inside.*

Two things were inside. A black handle from a china tea cup and a copper colored medal the size of a fifty-cent piece with a string through a hole at the top. One side had strange carvings and symbols. The back was like the inside of a spoon – slick and deep. Her thumb popped into the depression. Slid back and forth. Felt at home. Maddy smiled. Her secret charm.

Zach called out, "Hey, look what I found."

Maddy flipped the necklace over her head, tugged on her jersey, and dropped the pendant inside.

Zach flopped down next to her, string at something in his hand.

"What did you find?" Maddy asked.

"A brass button." Zach spit on it. Rubbed it clean.

"Probably just an overall button."

"Nuh-uh," Zach muttered. "This is a button from a Union Army uniform. I should know, I have to polish mine all the time." Zach looked over and saw the cigar box on Maddy's lap. "What'cha got there?"

"A box with a China tea cup handle."

"Let me see. Cool. Where'd ya get it?"

"From the house."

"Tell you what. Let's put the knife and my button in the box too. Our Drake House finds. And then let's not tell anyone about them, just yet. Okay?"

Maddy reached under her shirt. Her thumb found the smoothrubbing charm. "Sure."

Chapter Four

"Zach, time to get up," his mother called. "Your father will be here in half an hour."

"Aaargh," Zach groaned, rolling over for a few more minutes of sleep.

"I put your uniform out for you and I made you a nice breakfast. I don't want you gorging on junk food. And did you charge your cell phone?"

"Yes, Mother."

Zach leaned his elbow on the concession booth counter, propped his chin in his hand, and panned the ten soccer fields swarming with kids in bright colored uniforms. Now that the first games had started, the lines had shortened and he had a moment to himself.

What about those things we found last week, he wondered. *A handle to a tea cup and a brass army uniform button. How do they go together with the heart and the knife?*

Two fields over and one field back, he saw girls in green and white uniforms. Maddy's team. "Be right back!" he called to his father and the other two volunteers.

As he got closer he could make out Maddy on the sidelines. Her teammates frantically charged back and forth across the field. Maddy was absorbed in nipping a hangnail from her left index finger. The coach shouted something in her direction. Maddy looked up as if to say, "Who, me?" She dragged herself over to the scorer's table and waited for her teammate to come off the field.

She had barely jogged to her position when a forward from the team in blue blurred toward her dribbling the ball. Next to Zach, a gray-haired man who barely came to his shoulder, shouting, "Mark her, Maddy! Stick with her, girl!"

I bet that's her grandfather, Zach thought.

Maddy dashed toward the sprinting forward.

"Force her wide, Maddy!" the goalie shouted.

Maddy cut a nasty look at the keeper, her friend Neela. *I know what I'm supposed to do*, Maddy thought.

The glance cost her a step. Maddy ran hard to catch up. Five strides later she had to slide and kick the ball out of bounds. Corner kick. The girl in blue carefully placed the ball in front of the corner flag. Maddy's teammates shuffled and pushed to get in position.

The goalie barked orders. "Mark number 16. Karen, get on her. Julie, duck a little, I can't see."

The kicker launched a high floating ball into the churning mob in front of the goal. The goalie ran out, leaped to grab the ball. Number 16 sprang up for a header. They smashed together then bounced apart. The goalie tucked the ball to her body and landed on her side. She didn't get up.

"My shoulder," she moaned. "Ow! It hurts."

The coach ran onto the field. The girls from both teams sat on the grass. Maddy bit her lip while the coach gently coaxed Neela into a sitting position. Maddy was close enough to hear her friend crying softly, "Hurts! It hurts."

The coach and Neela's dad helped her to her feet then locked hands to form a seat. Neela hooked her good arm around her father's neck and they carried her off the field. Players and spectators clapped. On the sidelines the coach took Neela's gloves then scanned the remaining players.

"Maddy!" he called, holding out the gloves. "You're in goal."

"Me?" Maddy gasped, sliding her hand under her jersey till her thumb found the familiar smoothness of her secret charm. "I don't know how–"

"Just do it. Someone has to."

And I'm the least loss to the team, Maddy thought to herself as she worked her fingers into the goalie gloves, warm and wet with sweat.

"Can do, Maddy. I know you can," a voice called from the sidelines.

Sure, Grampa. Sure. Maddy thought. *Easy for you to say. And who's the red headed guy next to Grampa. Oh no. It's Zach. What's he doing here dressed like a soldier? I don't need any more people to watch me make a fool of myself. Aargh! Here they come down the right side.*

"Pick her up, Karen," Maddy shouted to her right defender. "Ride her off. Don't let her get to the middle." Out of the corner of her eye, she saw a blue shirt coming down the left side.

"Cross! Watch the cross!" Zach yelled.

The dribbler's not going to shoot. Not from that angle, Maddy thought. So she broke for the far side of the net just as the pass reached the open player. The shot screamed low to the corner. Maddy dove. The ball pounded hard into her gut. Save.

Cheering. People shouting. Great. *But I can't breathe. What's happening to me? I'm dying.*

The coach rolled Maddy onto her back and lifted her by the waist band of her shorts. "You just got the wind knocked out of you. You'll be fine. What a save! You were great."

Maddy sucked in air. Thinking. Trying to say, "It's great that I was great. Now I just want to go home."

"So, if we can hold them for another ten minutes, we get a win. Our first for the season. Hang on, kid. How did you know to anticipate that cross?"

Maddy staggered to her feet, shrugged. "Just did."

After the game, teammates filed by Maddy.

"Nice job."

"Way to go."

"Awesome."

That's different, Maddy thought. *Never had all that attention before.* Grabbing a juice bag from a cooler, Maddy punched in her straw, took a long sip, and went looking for her friend.

Neela slouched on a camp chair, an ice bag on her shoulder. Her father knelt in front of her. Her mother, in a bright orange Indian sari, held a damp cloth to her daughter's forehead. Normally as dusky skinned as her parents, Neela had paled to the color of light caramel.

"You okay?" Maddy asked.

Neela nodded. "You did good."

Maddy shrugged. "Somebody had to do it."

Mr. Patel stood and faced Maddy. "Neela is tough. She will be back in goal next Saturday."

"Sure hope so," Maddy replied.

Crossing midfield, Maddy's grandfather shouted, "Like I said, you were just great! I swear, you're a natural."

Zach, beside him, added, "Yeah, great saves!"

The older man looked at Zach. "You must know my granddaughter. From school, right?" Zach nodded. Checking out Zach's blue, Union Army uniform, he added, "Did I miss a parade or something?"

Zach blushed. "No, I–

Maddy broke in. "Uh, Grampa and Zach, this is Mr. and Mrs. Patel. They're our neighbors. And Neela, our goalie, is my best friend."

Turning to the Patel family, she said, "This is my grandfather, Pete Cooper, and that's Zach."

"Oh, geez, honey," Pete said to Neela, "I hope you're okay? You sure took a lick out there." Looking at the parents, he added, "She's tough, I can tell. She'll be back in a hurry."

Mr. Patel nodded.

"I know you from school," Zach said to Neela. "Don't you do a special dance when we have international day and stuff?"

Mrs. Patel nodded. "Neela is expected to know our traditional dances."

Neela rolled her eyes.

"Uhm, gotta go," Maddy said. "See you at practice, Neela."

"Nice to meet you," Pete said.

On the way to the parking lot, Pete wrapped his arm around Maddy's shoulder. "It won't be long and you'll be the starting goalie. You bet."

"Me? I'm no good."

"Not from what I saw," Pete replied. "You're a natural."

"How do you know? You never played soccer."

"It's your instincts. You knew what to do without any training. Imagine what you could do with some good coaching. It could happen. I'm telling you. It could happen."

"Yeah, and you're quick," Zach said. "Maybe you don't run fast but you move like lightning."

Maddy looked at Zach. "I don't want to be goalie. Neela's our keeper. I wouldn't do that to her. Besides she's my best friend," adding in a small voice, "my only friend."

"If I had a best friend," Zach said, "he'd want me to do as good as I could in... whatever. Period."

Next to her grandfather's car, Maddy paused to hold her stomach. "I don't feel so good." She went to one knee and retched. "I need to lie down."

"My house is right over there," Zach said, pointing to a group of apartment buildings on the far side of the soccer complex. "She can lie down there for a while. My mom won't mind."

"Are you sure?" Pete asked.

Chapter Five

MADDY LAY ON ZACH'S couch, her feet elevated, a last bite of toast and jelly on the way to her mouth.

"You're getting color back in your cheeks, honey," Zach's mother said.

"Sorry to bother you like this, Mrs. Andress," Grampa said.

"Just call me Allison, Mister–?"

"Pete's fine for me."

"Well, no problem, Pete. Actually I enjoy meeting new people – nice people like you and Zach's girlfriend."

Zach looked at Maddy. Maddy looked at Zach. Both shook their heads.

"Not," Zach sputtered.

Maddy frowned. "As if."

"You got to be careful what you say around young people these days," Pete chuckled. "You almost got Maddy sick to her stomach again."

Maddy sat up. Looked around. Noticed stacks of DVDs next to the TV. "Wow, you guys sure must like to watch movies."

"Oh no, not me. Not so much. It's Zach who's the movie nut. He'll watch a movie over and over."

"Mother!" Zach said. "I'm not just watching movies. I'm studying them so I can make them some day."

"You watch a movie more than once?" Maddy asked. "Once I know what's going to happen I don't want to see it again."

"Not me. I'll watch a movie again and again. Sometimes I back up and replay a scene till I know everything about it."

"Like what?" Pete asked.

"Like sound. Sometimes I'll turn my back and play a scene and just listen for the audio. Once for the words. Once for the music. Once for the sound effects." Warming up to his subject, Zach licked his lips and pushed on. "And sometimes I watch a movie with sound turned off and watch the edits and camera angles and lighting and all that. Haven't you ever done that?"

Maddy pursed her lips and rolled her eyes.

"Well, it's not weird," Zach explained, "it's what you have to know if you want to make movies."

"Zach thinks he's going to make a movie about the Drake House, Grandpa."

"How do you know about the old Drake House?" Pete asked.

"His father's restoring it," Allison said.

"Well, how about that," Pete said, leaning back, crossing his legs and wrapping his hands around his knee. "I grew up around here." Pete nodded as if agreeing with himself. "I've been interested in the place since I was a kid. I heard of a woman who was supposed to be a direct descendant of the original pioneers. Word is, she was born in that house."

"Really?" Zach said. "She still around?"

"Naw. She died a few years back. I never met her but I heard stories from people who knew her. That, and a lot of historical documents down to the township hall that tell all about Benjamin Drake and his family."

Zach looked at Maddy. He raised an eyebrow – *Should we tell him about our finds?*

Maddy shrugged – *I don't care*. Then she explained. "We found an old knife blade and some other stuff at the Drake Farm and Zach thinks he can make a movie out of it."

"An old knife, you say?" Pete asked.

Zach nodded. "And a Union army button from a uniform. And Maddy found a tea cup handle. And there was a heart carved in the barn that said NH and MD forever."

"There's gotta be a story here," Pete replied.

"Oh no," Maddy moaned. "Don't get Grampa rolling. Once he starts making up stories you'll never hear the end of it."

"That's just what I need," Zach said. "I pretty much know how you're supposed to make a movie but I don't know how to write a script. Can you help me write the screenplay?"

"You, bet," Pete replied. "Look, son, don't make a big mystery of it. A script's just a story put to pictures. How you write it down is like a play where you tell what each actor says."

"So, you'll help me?" Zach asked.

"You bet."

About the Author

Joe Novara, a retired corporate trainer and writing instructor, is a contributing author to the Storyshares library.

About the Publisher

Story Shares is a nonprofit focused on supporting the millions of teens and adults who struggle with reading by creating a new shelf in the library specifically for them. The ever-growing collection features content that is compelling and culturally relevant for teens and adults, yet still readable at a range of lower reading levels.

Story Shares generates content by engaging deeply with writers, bringing together a community to create this new kind of book. With more intriguing and approachable stories to choose from, the teens and adults who have fallen behind are improving their skills and beginning to discover the joy of reading. For more information, visit storyshares.org.

Easy to Read. Hard to Put Down.

Notes